Lois Golding

Tubbie Teddies
The Seaside Holiday

Illustrated by Rachel Dewick

Scholastic Publications Ltd.,
10 Earlham Street, London WC2H 9RX, UK

Scholastic Inc.,
730 Broadway, New York, NY 10003, USA

Scholastic Tab Publications Ltd.,
123 Newkirk Road, Richmond Hill,
Ontario L4C 3G5, Canada

Ashton Scholastic Pty. Ltd.,
PO Box 579, Gosford, New South Wales,
Australia

Ashton Scholastic Ltd.,
165 Marua Road, Panmure, Auckland 6,
New Zealand

First published by Scholastic Publications Limited, 1989
Text copyright © Scholastic Publications Ltd, 1989
Illustrations copyright © Leo Graphics UK Limited, 1989

ISBN 0 590 76104 8
All rights reserved
Made and printed in Hong Kong

Typeset by AKM Associates (UK) Ltd,
Ajmal House, Hayes Road, Southall, London.

Lois Golding

Tubbie Teddies
The Seaside Holiday

Illustrated by Rachel Dewick

Hippo Books
Scholastic Publications Limited
London

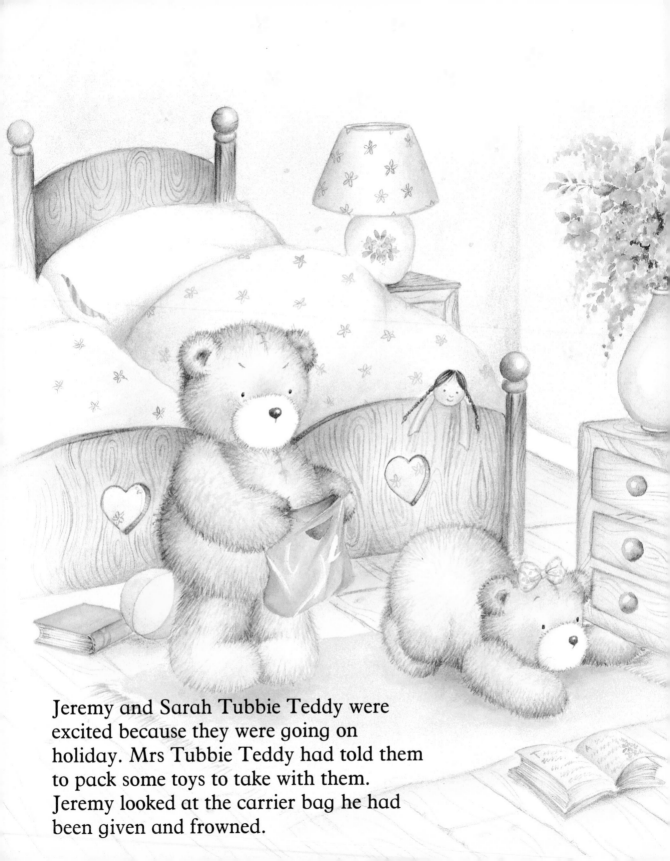

Jeremy and Sarah Tubbie Teddy were
excited because they were going on
holiday. Mrs Tubbie Teddy had told them
to pack some toys to take with them.
Jeremy looked at the carrier bag he had
been given and frowned.

"My toys won't go in that silly little bag. There's my train set and lines, my cricket bat . . ."
"I'm only taking Mary-Anne because she might feel lonely if I leave her behind," said Sarah.
"Fancy taking a rag doll!" scoffed Jeremy.

Mrs Tubbie Teddy came into the bedroom.
"Aren't you ready yet?"
"I am," said Sarah.
Mrs Tubbie Teddy looked at the toys lying
all over the floor and sighed. "I suppose
you can't make up your mind, Jeremy?"

Jeremy started pushing his train set into
the bag. "I want to take this, and these . . ."
Mrs Tubbie Teddy laughed. "You won't
want all those toys, Jeremy. Just bring your
buckets and spades, and a picture book
each in case it rains, and be outside in five
minutes."

Carrying their picture books and buckets
and spades they hurried downstairs. Mr
Tubbie Teddy was putting suitcases into
the back of the car. Mrs Tubbie Teddy
came out with Baby.

"I'll strap Baby into her seat. Sarah and Jeremy, you get in and fasten your safety belts," said Mrs Tubbie Teddy.
"Then we're off to the seaside," smiled Mr Tubbie Teddy.

They were going to stay with Auntie Jane.
After a long drive through the countryside
Mr Tubbie Teddy pulled up outside her
house. Sarah and Jeremy jumped out of the
car as soon as it stopped.

"Hello Auntie!" they shouted as they started running along the path leading to the beach. "We want to go down to the sea!"

"I'll see you again when you're hungry," laughed Auntie Jane.

When Jeremy and Sarah reached the beach they saw lots of mothers and fathers playing games with their children.
The tide was going out and the sand was nice and damp.

"I'm going to make a sandcastle!" cried Jeremy, filling his bucket with sand and pressing it down with his paws.
"Me too!" said his sister.

They worked very hard making a lovely
castle.

"Now we must collect some shells for the windows and doors," said Sarah.

When the castle was finished they stood
back and admired it.

"It's the best sandcastle we've ever made," said Jeremy. "If Daddy comes down to the beach with his camera we'll ask him to take a photograph."

Next to the castle was a little rock pool.
"If we dig a trench round the castle we
could turn it into a moat," Sarah said.
"What a good idea," agreed Jeremy
dashing to the pool. "Look at the starfish
and all those crabs in the water."
"Look out!" cried Sarah. "One of the
crabs is going to nip your toes!"

"Ouch!" said Jeremy, who had stepped into the water in his excitement.
He shook the little creature off and all the other crabs scuttled away under the stones.

"Oh no," wailed Sarah. "Just look at those boys!"
Jeremy looked round to see two boys jumping on their sandcastle.

"Let's chase them!" he cried, as the boys ran away. The boys soon disappeared. Jeremy and Sarah were very sad because their castle had been spoilt.

They decided to go and paddle in the sea.
They popped seaweed and threw pebbles
into the sea, making them bounce on the
water.

Sarah suddenly dug her brother in the ribs.
"Look over there! Those nasty boys are
sunbathing and they haven't seen us."

"Let's fill our buckets with water," said
Jeremy with a grin.
"What for?" asked Sarah.
"You'll see," replied Jeremy.

When the buckets were full they crept
along to where the two boys were dozing in
the sun.
"You tip your bucket over that one's feet
and I'll do the same to the other,"
whispered Jeremy.

Quick as a flash the buckets were emptied.
The two boys jumped up with their feet all
wet.
"Hey! What's going on?" shouted one of
them.
"That's for spoiling our sandcastle,"
replied Jeremy.

The boy's mother who was sitting close by looked puzzled until Jeremy and Sarah explained what had happened.
"It serves John and Joe right for being so mean," said their mother. "Now shake paws and say you're sorry."

The two boys really were sorry and after playing catch with a big beach ball, all four agreed to be friends.
Just then Mr Tubbie Teddy and Auntie Jane arrived.

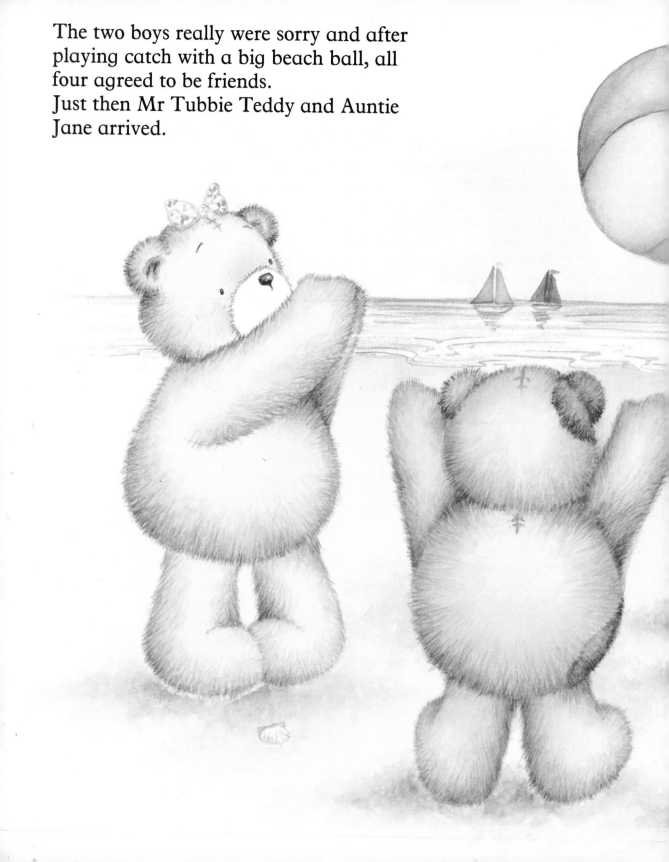

"Aren't you hungry?" asked Auntie Jane. "Starving," admitted Jeremy. "But we've had so many adventures we forgot about dinner."

"Say goodbye to your friends," said Mr
Tubbie Teddy. "You can meet again this
afternoon."

"Cheerio for now," grinned Jeremy.
"This afternoon we'll make the biggest
sandcastle in the world," said Sarah.
"Great!" replied John and Joe.

"We're going to have a lovely holiday,"
said Sarah as they walked back to Auntie
Jane's house.
"We always do," agreed Jeremy.